IVAN THE TERRIBLE;

OR,

DARK DEEDS OF NIGHT.

ILLUSTRATED WITH NUMEROUS ENGRAVINGS.

LONDON:
NEWSAGENTS' PUBLISHING COMPANY, 147, FLEET STREET, E.C.
1866.

IVÁN THE TERRIBLE;
OR, DARK DEEDS OF NIGHT.

IVAN BINDS HIMSELF TO THE SORCERER.—*See page 3.*

CHAPTER I.

IVAN THE TERRIBLE—THE MIDNIGHT STRUGGLE IN THE DARK ROOM OF THE VILLAGE INN—THE POISONED DAGGER—DEATH OF THE FRENCH SPY—THE WARNING VOICES.

OUR story belongs to the later years of the reign of King James II. The opening scene is laid among the hills and mountains of Cornwall close beside the sea.

It was a night of terrible storm, such as is seldom seen beyond the limits of the tropics.

It seemed as if the constant and vivid sheets of lightning would rend the very rocks and hills, while the thunder crashed over head in deafening peals.

The rain, heavy, and like a deluge, poured from the dark, storm-laden clouds without intermission, covering in a short space of time the whole face of the country with water.

The Vale of Glenloch was within sight of the sea, and its heavy, storm-crested billows could be plainly heard rolling upon the dark rock-bound coast with dull and regular roar.

No. 1.

The little town of Redfern could be seen dark and shadowy in the distant landscape.

The lights of the few dwellings in the vale were extinguished, and the inhabitants seemed to have sought their beds to escape the fury of the tempest.

The ale-house was the only dwelling that was open, and from the noise of songs and the clatter of voices, breaking often into oaths, that issued from it, showed that a numerous company were assembled.

In the tap-room were many drunken wreckers, coast guardsmen, and idle tramps, who, with hot brandy and rum, were regaling themselves to their heart's content.

In the parlour also were a party of gentlemen who had been overtaken by the storm, and sought shelter there, their horses still standing under a large shed in the stable yard.

But while these were thus amusing themselves below, and striving, by the free use of ardent liquor, to sustain the courage of which the storm had partly deprived them, a terrible scene was occurring in the room above.

ubscribers wishing to possess a superior impression of the magnificent Engraving given away with this Number can have one, printed on fine paper, by forwarding Five Stamps to the Office, 147, Fleet Street.

It was a conflict between two deadly enemies—*a duel in the dark!*

Two travellers, both unattended, had arrived at the " Green Dragon " during the evening.

They did not come together; one came at seven, and the other at nine o'clock, and each, after partaking of refreshments, had been shown to his bed-chamber and retired to rest.

Their rooms were far apart, although on the same floor; a very large ante-chamber, damp, unspeakably dark and empty, divided them, and served as a common entrance into both apartments.

A man, scarce distinguishable in the darkness, issued silently from one of the chambers, and groping his way to the door of the ante-room, which opened on to the landing, carefully closed and locked it.

He was in his night clothes, and crept on his hands and knees. A dagger was tightly clenched between his teeth!

He listened!

"Now is the moment for revenge !" he whispered to himself. " This poison-tipped weapon shall pierce his vile heart! I have tracked him long, and now he is mine! Yes, mine! dead or alive !"

He peered through the darkness, and stealthily approached the door of the opposite chamber.

He gently turned the handle. It was locked.

He probed for the key, and thought to turn it in the lock with a very small but powerful pair of pincers, but the key had been removed.

He crept back to his room, and shortly returned with a skeleton key.

He peeped into the keyhole.

A fierce, fiery, and tiger-like eye met his own.

He could distinctly hear heavy, suppressed, and painful breathing within the chamber as of some wild and ferocious animal.

The fierce and fiery eye seemed to chill his very marrow.

At that moment a tremendous clap of thunder crashed over the old inn, and shook it to its very foundation.

With the dagger still between his teeth, he crept like a cat towards his own room, the door of which he had left open to enable him to see how to unlock the apartment of his victim.

A flash at this moment lit up the whole place, and then the darkness seemed more profound; but the momentary light showed him that the door of his own chamber was closed.

He felt as if he had been watched.

Something, whether mortal or immortal, was near him, but who, or what, or where he knew not.

Upon his hands and knees, he made a complete circle around him with his dagger, but its point met with no resistance.

He moved hither and thither, but with the same result.

His arm passed rapidly through the air in every direction, but the space appeared vacant.

" 'Tis only imagination," he thought; yet a cold, clammy moisture stood on his brow.

His breathing became oppressive, and a feeling of horror seemed to harrow up his very soul.

He listened. A slight, soft and repressed sigh was heard.

He turned, and two fiery eyes met his gaze.

He crouched still lower like a panther when about to bound upon its prey.

He was face to face with some unseen, unknown, but deadly enemy.

'Twas now a question of life or death, for he could plainly hear the hard breathing of his foe. But the eyes had disappeared.

It was no time for thought, he must take immediate action.

" If I do but only prick him with the point of this poisoned dagger he dies !" was his thought.

He crept inch by inch to where he fancied his foe must be, and struck a fierce blow, but his dagger's point entered on the hard floor.

He crept from corner to corner but saw not the fiery, fearful eyes, but as he was about to re-enter the chamber he saw them again.

He rose to his feet, and bounded towards them dagger in hand, but in the darkness a piece of furniture caught his foot and he stumbled.

In an instant the deadly dagger was wrenched from him.

He was grasped by the throat with a vice-like grip, and a struggle ensued that was fearful, awful, deadly.

One or both must die !

Though violently struggling, and twisting and twining in their deadly embrace, they rolled about upon the floor without the slightest noise or uproar, for both were in their stockinged feet.

No words were spoken, but the hard breathing of both told too well how herculean and desperate were their efforts.

The longer the struggle lasted the more fierce and terrible shone the fiery eyes.

They glared in the darkness like burning coals; then they suddenly flashed with devil-like brilliancy.

An arm is upraised ! There is a stifled shriek—a heavy fall —and the struggle is over !

The poisoned dagger had pierced the heart of its owner !

His body lies upon the floor without a moan or groan.

"Ha, ha ! Goutril ! you sought your fate, and have met it !" hissed the voice of him whose red, flashing eyes seemed to gloat over the gory corpse at his feet. So you could not rest in France, eh, but you must follow me to my native land. Ha, ha ! the biter bit ! There you lay, my fine gentleman, and when I choose to honour France with a flying visit again I think Monsieur Goutril or his spies and detectives will never molest me again."

So saying, he leaned over the body, and felt his victim's heart.

"Dead as a door-nail !" he said, with a low, chuckling laugh. " *I never miss !* It matters little what weapon I use, by night or day, my aim is true."

" My aim is true !" re-echoed a sepulchral voice.

CHAPTER II.

THE BOND OF BLOOD—IVAN THE TERRIBLE SELLS HIMSELF BOTH BODY AND SOUL—THE MAGICIAN'S FATAL POWER —THE HAUNTED CAVERN.

THE villain stood in the dark chamber, and stared about him with the fierceness and ferocity of a tiger.

"What voice was that I heard ?" he half whispered to himself.

" The voice of Dreadnought."

"Dreadnought ?" asked the villain. " What brings *thee* here ?"

" Dost tremble, then ? 'Tis not the first time we have met."

" Tremble ! No, not I ; I tremble at nothing," the dark villain said, with scorn.

" Dost know the year, the week, the day ?" asked the unseen, unknown speaker, in a hoarse whisper.

" Yes, the day and the hour !" was the fierce, hissing, sounding retort.

" Then, art thou ready for the compact ?"

" The bond of blood ?"

" Yes."

" I am."

" Then follow me."

" What, through the assembled company below ?"

" No, down the back stairs, through the stables ; mount your horse, and follow me."

The murderer did as he was bidden.

It seemed as if the voice of him that spoke had a supernatural influence over him.

He mounted his horse and followed.

The winds screamed and howled around him as he noiselessly left the stable yard.

Dark birds of night—ominous, unclean birds—circled round his head.

He perceived before him in the darkness the tall, gaunt figure of an old man, whose long, silvery locks were blown about in the breeze.

He carried a long staff, with which he motioned to the clouds, as if bidding them drift away.

At his side walked a panther!

It was tame, and gambolled about like a kitten.

Ever and anon, however, it would turn upon the horseman following, and with flashing eyes, and long, glistening fangs, would growl.

"Quiet, Demon," the old man said, in soothing tones.

And the fierce-looking, active, agile panther was quieted on the instant.

They reached a dark and lonely glen.

The villain followed as if spell-bound.

They wound their way among the rocks and hills, and arrived at the entrance of a cave.

The horseman followed.

He did not dismount, but stooped his head, so as not to hurt it against the projecting rocks.

He dismounted, and some unknown one ushered him into a spacious rocky chamber.

Dreadnought the Wizard sat upon his throne.

Around him were mysterious symbols, ornaments, and weapons of various kinds.

He had a magic wand in his right hand.

The black, silky, and fierce-looking panther lay at his feet.

The murderer entered!

He was a tall, powerfully-built fellow, fierce and ugly.

His whiskers and beard were long, shaggy, and untrimmed.

He strode into the apartment like one who feared neither God nor devil.

His hands were red with gore.

"What want ye with me?" he asked, in a rough loud tone.

"To fulfil your promise."

"And what was that?"

"To bind yourself to me in life or death as a willing slave!"

"And if I do not, what then?"

"What then, Ivan?" laughed the old man in derision, "You die upon the spot."

"You talk bravely, Dreadnought, for an old man."

"Old as I may be, I am still your master! Let me but give the signal, earth shall open beneath your feet, and you will be engulphed in a caldron of boiling vitriol."

"Ha! ha!" laughed Ivan, "you would attempt to frighten me, eh?"

"Frighten you, Ivan? No, you are surnamed the Terrible; but who made you so? Was it not my mystic power that gathered you the band you have? What would you be without Eagle-Eye, the Shark, the Wolf, or others of your followers?"

"And what is to be the price?"

"A charmed life."

"But that has a spell?"

"Which, if broken, you are lost!"

"And what is it that is so potent and powerful?"

"A simple maid!"

"A woman, say you? ha! ha!" laughed Ivan, "am I to be conquered by a woman, a mere girl? Why, you mock me."

"Did I mock you the night before you were to be hung, not long ago? or when you were hunted through the whole country like a fox?"

"No; you behaved the friend."

"What say you to the compact, then?"

"Read it," said Ivan, with indifference, "*I may as well live a little longer*," he said, in a tone of unearthly melancholy.

The old magician drew forth a parchment, and read as follows:—

"Ivan, surnamed the Terrible, binds himself as a willing slave."

"I do."

"To serve me, his lawful master, when required."

"I do."

"In all things I may command."

"I do."

"For which, by my spells and power, I charm his life against all, save a simple girl, for the term of ten years."

"Correct," said Ivan, who treated the matter as a very good joke, and could not help bursting out into a loud laugh.

"Will you sign?" Dreadnought asked.

"I will. Where is the pen and ink?" he asked, indifferently.

"The ink is here," he said, approaching Ivan, whose arm was bared.

At the same moment he touched a vein with a lancet, and caught the blood in a bowl!

"Here is ink enough, I think," said Dreadnought, with a grim smile. "Come, dip your pen in this," he said, "and sign."

While he held the lamp for Ivan to sign the awful deed his eyes glared like two bright streams of green fire.

Ivan took the pen.

His hand began to tremble violently.

He was seized with a sudden chilliness about the heart and a dizziness in the head.

He signed the deed!

At that moment loud peals of thunder were heard rolling overhead, the panther roared, and lightning flashed through a fissure in the rock.

Ivan's senses reeled! From some unknown cause he fell to the floor.

Dreadnought stood over his victim with a laugh of triumph, as he muttered again and again,

"The deed is done! He is mine! he is mine! Aye, both body and soul!"

He had scarcely uttered the last words when screams both fierce and frightful were re-echoed through the dark, dank, and spacious cavern.

Fires of various hues seemed to glow upon the walls, while phosphorescent and aerial forms glided to and fro noiseless and horrible, or at a motion of the magician's wand would dance around the prostrate victim.

CHAPTER III.

BANDY BOB'S TERROR—THE DISCOVERY OF THE MURDER— BILL BARRY THE THIEF-TAKER— THE ARREST OF CAPTAIN BLUE JACKET.

'TWAS late ere the storm abated, and the revellers in the "Green Dragon" were not inclined to leave.

Bandy Bob, the groom and pot-boy, was yawning in the chimney corner of the tap-room.

He was about to retire to bed when a horseman arrived at the inn and desired a night's lodging.

He was accommodated, and his horse provided for.

"There's no mistake about this 'ere 'orse," said Bob, as he rubbed the animal down with a wisp of straw. "They may talk as they pleases, but it's a downright pleasure to do a good turn for a hanimal like this 'un. I've been in Lunnon many a year, and *I* never seed a finer 'orse, and no mistake. King James couldn't sport a finer nag, *I* know. Lor!" said Bob, stroking down the noble beast, "wouldn't *I* like to have a ride on 'im? Crickey! wouldn't it be a go?"

It must be confessed that Bob's admiration for the animal arose from the fact that the gallant-looking owner thereof had tossed him a crown, a coin of the realm which Master Bob had seldom seen of late.

When he retired to bed the horseman had told Bob, on the sly, that after the horse had been well groomed he must re-saddle it ready for instant use.

"For you see, my lad," said the horseman, "I may want to start off at a moment's notice, so, therefore, you need not trouble yourself about the stable-door. Leave it open, there's no fear of Jupiter running away."

The company in the parlour and tap were roaring out their songs and toasts, and everything bid fair that they would continue to do so until morning.

Bandy Bob, therefore, took a long draught of porter, kissed the barmaid, who was half asleep, and went up to bed yawning.

In a few moments he came downstairs again in his stockinged feet, looking the very picture of fear and alarm.

His eyes were staring out of their sockets.

His hair stood on end, and he trembled in every limb.

He rushed into the parlour, and tumbled head over heels among the company, knocking over the card-table and all the money, bottles and glasses thereon.

He was well cuffed and kicked for his pains, and lay sprawling in the middle of the room, while all the company, indignant and noisy, stood around.

His moans and groans were incessant, and to all questions he simply answered,

"Oh, lor! Oh, gents! Oh, it's a 'orrible sight is that 'ere."

"What is horrible, you ragamuffin?" asked one, kicking poor Bob in the ribs. "Speak, I tell you, what has frightened you?"

"Have you seen a ghost?" asked one.

"Oh, more 'orrible than that."

"What *have* you seen, then?" asked another. "Speak out on the instant or we will half kill you."

"Murder, gents, murder!" blubbered Bob. "Oh, let me get away out of this ere 'ouse; it'll turn us all grey. Oh, go up stairs; that furrin-looking gent, as came to night, is in the ante-room, dead and cold as mutton!"

"Murder?"

"Dead?" asked several, in a breath, with looks of unfeigned horror and surprise.

"Who could have done it?" asked several.

"Let's go up and examine the room," said one burly fellow, with the air of a man who had been accustomed to witness deeds of violence. "Don't make a noise; only one or two, mind, not all of ye; cock your pistols and follow me."

The burly red-faced man, pistol in-hand, led the way,

He was followed by several gentlemen sword in hand.

They crept up stairs carefully and quietly.

He who led the way, to the astonishment of the others, pulled a small dark lantern from his capacious pocket.

He put his finger to his lips in token of silence.

His caution was heeded.

The ante-room was reached.

To the horror of all, they saw a murdered man lying in a pool of blood, stone dead, and cold.

The neighbouring rooms were examined.

They were tenantless.

"Stay a moment," said the burly gentleman, lantern in hand, "we must examine further."

Without speaking another word, he peeped into the key-hole of a room adjoining.

The key had been taken out.

"We must go over the kitchen roof," he whispered, "and get in at the window!"

No sooner said than done.

With the quietness of a cat, the burly fellow, followed by three determined and resolute gentlemen, got upon the kitchen roof.

The bed-room window was slowly, softly opened.

The burly leader and his followers dexterously entered the apartment.

A shot was fired by him that lay in bed!

One of the gentlemen, just in the act of getting in at the window, uttered a cry of pain.

He fell off the kitchen roof into the yard below.

The sleeper, whoever he was, had taken accurate aim, but the moment he had fired the burly fellow fell flat upon the ground as if dead.

All was darkness.

The slumberer rushed towards the window with a loud laugh, and was about to jump out upon the roof, when the burly fellow and his followers seized him, and cast him to the floor with great violence.

"At last!" laughed the burly fellow, in triumph, as he and his companions pinioned the prostrate man.

"At last!" he repeated, turning on his dark lantern, and scanning the features of his captive. "I thought I couldn't be much mistaken."

"Is that *you?*" gasped the captive, in surprise, as he critically examined the one with the lamp. "What! Bill Barry?"

"Aye, my lad. Bill Barry, the thief-taker, at your service."

"What, are you the noted Bill Barry, the Bow Street-runner?" asked the gentlemen, in surprise.

"Yes, gents; no other, I can assure ye. I have 'wanted' this young gentleman for some time. I knowed as how he'd come this way this week to have a look at Lady Laura up at the Castle."

"Lady Laura?" they asked. "Why, what can this scoundrel want with a lady of title and quality?" they added, in indignant surprise. "You don't mean to say that he's impudence enough to address an earl's daughter?"

"Impudence enough, gents? Him? Lor' bless yer innercence! Why, this youth here, as looks so good-looking and simple, is the greatest cracksman on the king's highway, ain't you, my hearty, eh? But yer little game's over now, my lad."

"What's his name, then?"

"Blue Jacket—Captain Blue Jacket is the name he goes by—the biggest and daringest young scamp in the three kingdoms. He has a regular band under him, and they calls theirselves the 'Fly-by-Nights.' Oh, there's many on 'em, *I* can tell yer; but I hopes to have 'em all in less than a week or two. There'll be a fine hanging match at Tyburn, and no mistake."

This announcement of Bill Barry, the noted thief-taker, filled all with surprise, and none more so than Bandy Bob, the potman, who, more dead than alive, stood at the door, candle in one hand and a poker in the other.

At his heels was a nondescript crowd of servants, rustics and travellers, who had hurried to the scene, and stood looking on in bewilderment.

Blue Jacket spoke not a word, but frowned upon his captors.

He did not attempt to stir, for it was impossible to escape.

He was surrounded on all sides by angry men, who were narrating to each other all they had ever heard of the daring doings of the famous Blue Jacket and his band.

"That him? That Captain Blue Jacket?" asked Bob, shivering with fear. "Why he's stopped and upset many a good coach-load of gentlefolk 'tween here and Lunnon, as I knows well."

"Ah, won't he catch it now, eh?" grinned another.

"They won't string him up at Tyburn, oh, not in the least, I believe," said a third.

The pinioned robber was conveyed downstairs.

A light cart with two swift horses was in readiness below.

"We must take him to London. It won't do to trust him in any of the prisons hereabouts. He's broken gaol more than a dozen times, I can tell ye, young as he is; but he won't escape *this* time, or my name isn't Bill Barry. Besides," he added, with a wink, "there's a large reward offered for him, d'ye see?"

Without further preparations or delay Blue Jacket was placed in the cart, and Bob undertook to drive it, provided a sufficient guard of gentlemen would volunteer to accompany and escort the noted roadsman to the nearest gaol.

Bill Barry went to the stable to look for Blue Jacket's horse.

It had disappeared, but none knew how or whither.

The rain poured in torrents, but wrapped up in their over coats and cloaks, the cavalcade journeyed through the storm, highly delighted with their important capture, and firmly resolved that, come what might, they would not rest until they had seen the noted horseman heavily ironed and safely secured in the nearest county prison.

What happened there another chapter will quickly show us.

CHAPTER IV.

HARRY PERCY RESCUES A YOUNG LADY FROM DROWNING—GALLANT CONDUCT OF HANDSOME NED AND THE "FLY-BY-NIGHTS"—THE WATCHER—CAPTAIN BLUE JACKET—THE BOW STREET "FERRET."

THE night was dark and one could scarcely see the features of any one that might pass.

A very handsome and noble youth with his groom were

crossing Blackfriars bridge returning from a famous suburban theatre. It was between eleven and twelve o'clock.

They were passed by the frail, delicate form of a young girl about fourteen years of age.

She was sobbing loudly.

The young horseman was attracted by her grief, and followed her closely.

When she had arrived at the middle of the bridge she suddenly jumped over.

An awful splash was heard below.

The young horseman did not hesitate for a moment; he leaped off his steed, divested himself of his coat, vest and shoes, and jumped over the parapet of the bridge after her!

The servant was paralysed with astonishment.

Taking charge of the two horses he galloped down to the river's edge, tied them together, and looked for a small boat.

He found one and jumped in, but it was tied by a rope.

He tugged and tugged, but the rope broke not.

He had no knife!

He pulled at the boat with the energy of despair.

The rope snapped!

The servant fell back sprawling into the middle of the boat legs upward.

His young master, meanwhile, he could hear was splashing about and diving like a young seal.

The servant was impatient to go to the rescue.

He had but one oar, the other had been lost!

He attempted to row with this, but went round and round in the water like a whirligig.

The river was so black that, as it rolled by, it looked like a vast sea of ink.

Now and then a little wave arose and cast up its white spray.

The servant for a moment could see the white garment of the drowning girl and the head of his master above the dark water.

His young master shouted with the energy of despair.

"I see her! I see her! Help! help!"

With two brave strokes he reached the spot where her white garments had been seen.

In a second nought but his legs were visible.

He had dived deep!

One moment more he reappeared above the turgid waters.

He grasped the maiden by her long, luxuriant hair!

By this time the river bank was crowded by a mob of idlers that had been attracted to the spot.

"Bravo!" shouted some. "Well done, brave lad!" shouted others, as the desperate struggle for life or death continued, but no one attempted to render any assistance.

The servant with his one oar was fast losing confidence, for his boat was drifting away.

His master with his burden was boldly plunging one-handed to the shore, but he was fast going. A rattling in his throat and great dizziness was coming on.

He perceived his servant at a little distance from him, and shouted,

"Here, Darby! here!"

He disappeared!

A cry of horror was heard on shore.

Next moment Darby felt something clutch his oar.

It was his youthful master!

In an instant Darby clutched the hand as well as he could, but the weight of his master, now totally insensible, together with his prize, was too much for the little boat, and it almost capsized.

"Let go of her," Darby cried, "and save yourself."

This was shouted out so loudly that it aroused the youth from the delirious feelings that were fast mastering him.

"Let go, I say, let go! Save yourself!" Darby shouted, in despair.

"Never! We shall die together," the youth faintly answered.

"We are going, sir!—we must sink! Save yourself! Let her go! For God's sake, sir, save yourself!" Darby cried, and not without reason, for the boat was half capsized, and filling fast with water.

"No, no, save *her*, or let us die together," the brave youth sighed, and let go his hold.

It was an awful moment.

Darby could see the eyes of his young master staring wildly. His arm was raised above water, with fingers cramped, as if supplicating Heaven.

He disappeared beneath the inky tide.

Darby uttered a shout of horror.

"He is lost! he is lost!" he said, in tones of despair.

At that moment a six-oared boat darted past Darby like an arrow!

He gazed in wonder at the speed of the rowers.

They seized his young master by the hair of his head, and lifted him into the boat with as much ease as if he were but a child.

The maiden was also lifted into the boat, and they were rapidly pulling towards the shore when the shouts of Darby arrested their attention.

"Help, help! I'm sinking! Oh, help!"

Directing their swift craft towards him, one of the rowers threw out the boat-hook, which, fastening on to Darby's boat, soon drew it into shore.

The master, maid, and servant were saved!

"Bravo, gentlemen! bravo!" shouted the crowd, who clapped their hands in jubilee over the rescue.

"Bravo the devil!" answered one of the oarsmen, in disgust, as he shoved his way through the crowd. "A pretty set of vagabonds ye are, truly, to stand by and see a mere boy endanger his life for the sake of a poor girl, and here stand ye, a crowd of dirty and over-fed varlets, gaping on the while," answered one of those who had manned the boat.

"Come, come, Ned," whispered a companion, to him, in confidence, "don't have any talk with these ragamuffins. You know there are several on the look-out for us; a crowd is sure to attract some of the night watch. I know you haven't any idea of being lodged in Newgate so very soon after your late escape, so let us seek our horses and get away; we've done quite enough."

"True, Andy," Ned replied, "but before I go I'll learn the name of this gallant boy, and shake him by the hand too, if he were surrounded by all the officers in Bow Street."

So saying the one named Ned, who was a handsome-looking, gaily, flashily-dressed fellow, strode towards the brave boy, who, having now recovered, was leaning over and chafing the hands of the almost inanimate maid.

"What might your name be, my brave lad?" asked Handsome Ned, shaking him by the hand very heartily.

"Many, many thanks, kind sir, for preserving my life; but I think I have a card with me," said Harry, with a gay laugh.

So saying he produced a small card, and, by the light of a torch, Ned read:—

HENRY PERCY, JUN.
Percy House, and Glenloch Castle,
Cornwall.

"The youngest son of the earl," whispered Ned's companion.

"The devil! Why, then, this youngster is the brother of Lady Laura, Captain Blue Jacket's flame!" said Ned, in surprise.

"True; but who's the girl he's taken so much trouble to rescue from drowning?"

"I know not. A beautiful young creature, though, as ever lived, judging from her features."

"It might be well to inquire."

"There is a mystery here," answered Ned; "but let us away. I shall watch this young Percy and the unknown girl."

"It would be well to inform the captain of it."

"Oh, he's in Cornwall, love-making, ere this," said Ned, laughing. "We need not expect him in London for two weeks at least."

While they thus spoke in whispers, apart from the crowd, and made their way towards where their horses stood, they were watched and followed!

They knew not who it was that tracked them thus.

Yet as Ned and Andy mounted their horses they were joined by four companions, while a single man, hiding from the rays of an old oil lamp at the corner of a narrow street, whispered to a companion who was well concealed in the deep shadows of a doorway,

"So! so! werry good, Master Andy and Handsome Ned, so you and four others of the 'Fly-by-Nights' have been cheating the fishes of a supper, eh? Well, well, my jolly gentlemen, I'll follow you. There's *some* game up when six on ye get together, and no mistake!"

So spoke one who was well known as the Bow Street "Ferret!"

―――

CHAPTER V.

LIZZIE ASHTON—DARBY'S EXPEDITION—HIS FIGHT WITH THE SERVANTS—A SHOWER OF GOLD—RAGE OF COLONEL ASHTON—THE IMPENDING DUEL.

"DARBY, bring a hackney coach immediately," shouted young Harry Percy to his groom. "We must remove the girl at once, there are signs of life yet remaining. Lose not a moment."

"Fetch a doctor!" shouted one.

"Run and get a stretcher!" roared another in the crowd. "The girl is dying."

"Never mind expense," said a third "the young gentleman is rich, *he* don't mind a sovereign or two."

Despite all the noise of the gabbling crowd, young Harry knelt with the girl's head upon his knees, and chafed her hand and chest to restore animation.

Within a short time Darby returned with a hackney coach.

The girl was placed therein, and rapidly driven to the "King's Head" tavern, near St. Paul's church, a house which in those ancient days was a famous stopping-place for stage-coaches.

A doctor was sent for, by whose assistance the pale and beautiful girl, after much labour and many appliances, was soon restored to consciousness.

"Oh! my father!—my poor, poor father!" were her first words.

"Your father, dear sister?" Harry affectionately asked. "Where does he live? Oh! tell me on the instant that I may bring him hither."

For some time the girl could not speak, for her tears were flowing thick and fast.

Her snowy bosom heaved with such intense emotion, and she struggled so violently to conceal her sorrow that the kind old doctor shaded and averted his eyes from the painful scene.

"Your name, dear girl?" asked Harry, flushed with excitement. "Tell me on the instant, I pray you."

His words were uttered in such genuine tones of kindness that she looked at the speaker with ineffable looks of gratitude and love, as she murmured,

"Lizzie Ashton, 17, Palace Yard," and then fainted.

As she lay upon the snow-white bed, with her flowing hair, pale face and fevered coloured lips, Lizzie Ashton looked surpassingly beautiful.

"Poor child," whispered the kind landlady, and tenderly kissed her.

Meanwhile the doctor held a bottle to her nose, which seemed to revive her somewhat, and she muttered all manner of unintelligible things.

Master Darby, fancying that as *he* also had had a good ducking, the bottle might also do *him* some good, therefore slyly applied it to his own red nose, and took a long and hearty sniff.

The effect was instantaneous! It felt to Master Darby's nose like the pricking of a thousand pins and needles!

He coughed, got red in the face, tears ran out of his eyes, and his nose and mouth were puckered up in the most comical manner possible, ending in a terrific volley of quick and violent sneezings.

"Here, donkey," said Harry, who could not help laughing at the droll expression of his groom. "Hello, Darby, up to your tricks as usual, eh? Come, give over sneezing, sir, and

take this note immediately to No. 17, Palace Yard. Mount your horse, and gallop all the way as if the devil were after you!"

Darby did not much relish the ride, soaking wet as he was, and particularly because his wet clothes, coming in contact with his saddle seat, chafed him awfully, and made particular parts of his person red and raw with the exercise.

After twenty minutes of hard riding he stopped before the door of No. 17, Palace Yard. He knocked again and again.

It was now long past midnight, and all in that quiet, respectable and peaceful neighbourhood had been long a-bed.

At last an old porter opened the door, and was shivering and grumbling.

"Mr. Ashton?" asked Darby, also shivering in his wet clothes. "I want to see him immediately! It is a case of life or death!" he added.

"Good Heavens!" exclaimed the old porter. "Do you bring any good news of his daughter Elizabeth?"

"Yes."

"Give me the letter, then, *I* will take it," said the porter, with an eye to a possible five-pound note.

"No, you don't do *me* in that 'ere way," said Darby, with a chuckle and grin. "I delivers this 'ere letter myself."

"Why, but the colonel has gone to bed this two hours or more. He sleeps in the second floor front, and there hasn't been a light there for ever such a long time. He's fast asleep by this time, you musn't disturb him. Give me the letter, or I'll call the constable."

"You will, will yer?" said Darby, giving the crusty porter a slap in the jaw that knocked him sprawling in the passage. "Second floor front, eh, my joker, all right."

Next moment saw Darby flying up the stairs, unheeding the curses and howlings of the porter.

He jumped up the stairs four steps at a time.

There was a door ajar, and a light in the room.

He peeped in, and saw an old grey-headed man, who was weeping and kissing a miniature in great distress of mind.

He put the miniature by, and began to load his pistols.

"This must be the old 'un," thought Darby, and he boldly pushed open the door. "I come from Miss Ashton," he said, trembling, confronting the old man, and presenting the letter.

The colonel took the letter, and, growing deadly pale, gasped out,

"My daughter!"

Darby was by no means easy in mind, for the colonel's pistol was loaded, cocked, and mechanically presented at his head.

The colonel threw down the pistol, and tore open the letter.

A cold sweat oozed from his fine, manly and martial brow.

His very hair seemed to stand on end with excitement and fright.

"She lives! she lives!" he exclaimed aloud, "and your brave young master has saved her! Let me fly to her on the instant."

Putting his hand into a drawer with much haste he pulled out a handful of gold and threw it at the astonished Darby.

He next placed a brace of pistols in his breast, seized his hat, and rushed downstairs.

The porter who had followed Darby upstairs thought that he was entitled to some of the gold coin that lay scattered on the floor, and, without further invitation or ceremony, began to help himself to a few pieces.

This was more than Darby bargained for, he therefore laid violent hands on the porter, gave him, as he called it, "one, two for himself," and knocked him headlong downstairs.

By this time the whole household was aroused, but Darby very wisely took to his heels and left the house.

His horse was gone!

He did not know that the colonel had vaulted away upon it.

He called a hackney coach, however, and was driven back to the inn as fast as a two-horse conveyance could do it.

"There will be a devil of a stew over this, *I* know," said Darby, slapping and jingling the gold in his pockets. "There will be bloodshed before morning, or I am much mistaken in the ferocious old colonel."

He was not mistaken, however, as the sequel will shortly show.

CHAPTER VI.

THE FATAL BLOW—THE DUEL—THE DEATH—HARRY PERCY AND COUNT VINCENTO IN DEADLY COMBAT—THE VILLAIN'S DEATH—THE STRANGE AND AWFUL DISCOVERY—DARBY WANTS TO " BOX " SOMEBODY, IN ORDER " TO KEEP HIS HAND IN."

COLONEL ASHTON galloped towards the inn at St. Paul's churchyard at a terrific pace.

Darby's horse seemed to know the important errand he was on, and put forth all his powers.

The old colonel was dying to embrace his lost daughter and learn from her own lips the story of her wrongs and sufferings.

" Which is the ' King's Head ?' " he breathlessly inquired of an old night constable.

" That be it, sir," was the reply, " where thee sees a light, and shadows crossing the second-floor windows."

The old colonel jumped off his horse with the alacrity of a youth, and knocked loudly at the inn door.

It was opened by the good old landlord himself.

The colonel was as white as a sheet.

One beside him could hear the rapid palpitation of his heart.

He took the landlord's arm, muttering,

" Oh, if I were to find her dead !" and looking wildly, half-crazed with fear and anxiety.

At that moment the second story door was opened and a female voice was heard to exclaim, faintly, feebly, but repeatedly,

" Father ! oh, my father !"

" It is she !" exclaimed the colonel, with a face suddenly lit up with joy.

The old man, who a moment before was trembling like a leaf, sprang forward like a boy, and entered the chamber.

Without noticing any one else he threw himself upon his daughter's bed, exclaiming, with many tears,

" Oh, Lizzie, Lizzie ! my dear lost, darling daughter !"

It was quite a picture to see the father's rough, soldier-like face, with his grey beard and moustache, resting over and kissing the beautiful, pale, placid features of his long-lost child.

Harry Percy, with a noble delicacy of feeling, desired all to retire from the room, in order to allow father and daughter to indulge in mutual grief and joy.

The old colonel motioned young Harry Percy and the good landlord to remain, but all others retired.

When sufficiently recovered Lizzie Ashton, with many tears, told the story of her wrongs.

She had left her uncle's in Gloucestershire and was travelling in her own father's carriage towards London.

When fifty miles from home, and while the carriage was progressing over a lonely heath, it was stopped and attacked by three robbers on foot.

The postilion and footmen fought manly and bravely, but they were all overpowered and shot dead on the spot.

One of the robbers, whom the others called Count Vincento, and who appeared to be the leader, ordered his companions to act as postilion, and he himself jumped into the carriage, and told them to drive to London.

Frightened almost out of her wits the poor girl was stupefied, and could not utter a word.

This so-called Count Vincento confessed that he was nought else but a highwayman, and should not have acted as he had done except that he was in a great hurry to arrive in London in order to meet a certain celebrated outlaw surnamed Ivan the Terrible.

Not content with insulting and robbing the poor defenceless girl Count Vincento simply laughed at her misfortune and miseries ; he had cut off nearly all her curls, and because she wept bitterly at this treatment he opened the carriage door and thrust her out, penniless, lonely, and far away from home.

The colonel had listened thus far attentively to his daughter's words with a flushed face, and clenched teeth.

At the mere mention of the name of Count Vincento, how-

ever, he turned deadly pale, and sank into a chair from pure exhaustion.

The landlord attempted to say a word, but the colonel would not permit any interruption to his daughter's story.

She therefore proceeded to say that she travelled on both night and day to reach London as best she could, first selling one thing and then another in order to obtain both shelter and bread.

She had to submit to numberless insults and privations.

The gipsies hunted her for two days thinking to kidnap her among their tribe.

By hiding in the woods by day, however, and travelling by night, she eluded them ; but as she neared her journey's end her strength began to fail her. She was seized with frequent and violent weeping, her senses began to reel, she imagined that every man's hand was upraised, and ready to strike her.

Crossing Blackfriars Bridge strength and courage failed her. She had been for nights and days without lodging or food. In a fit of fear, alarm, and desperation she knew not what she did or where she was going. All consciousness was gone, and did not return until the moment when she found herself surrounded by a large mob of people, and reclining in the arms of her brave, noble, and gallant deliverer.

Harry Percy spoke not a word ; the story of the simple but beautiful girl filled his soul with sorrow. He wept, and willingly kissed the hand of the grateful girl as she stretched it forth to him.

" Vincento ! Count Vincento !" gasped the landlord. " Why he owes me——"

" I know him !" the colonel replied. " From my daughter's description I cannot mistake the scoundrel !" and as he said so he trembled in every limb.

" What kind of a carriage was it ?" eagerly asked the portly, rosy-faced landlord.

" The scoundrel called upon me a week ago," interrupted the colonel, " and said that he had been asked to deliver a letter from my brother in Gloucestershire, saying that my daughter had resolved to stay there a week longer ; that is now more than a month ago. His bearing was so unexceptional that I asked him if he would be so good as to convey back to my brother several valuable packages and parcels containing notes and specie. He willingly consented. I gave them to him. I have since had proof that he is a swindler, and a black-hearted scoundrel !"

" You must be mistaken in the person," said the landlord " Why, he lives in this very hotel !"

" What !" roared the colonel, " that scoundrel in this hotel ?"

" Yes, and has not yet returned home. Hark !"

Footsteps were heard upon the stairs.

" 'Tis Count Vincento himself," said the landlord. " I can tell by his creaking boots."

A mode of action was immediately agreed upon.

The old colonel hid himself in a large cupboard that was used as a wardrobe.

No one was visible within the room save the doctor, the landlord and Harry Percy.

Count Vincento was politely accosted on the stairs by the landlord with many bows, and was invited into the apartment.

He was a tall man, with dark whiskers and moustache, elegantly attired in the approved mode and fashion of the day.

His eyes were small, piercing and restless. There was an habitual sneer of half contempt half indifference upon his countenance, and his hands, though small and white, were powerful, sinewy, vice-like, and determined in the grip.

Young Percy was but a mere boy compared to him, yet there was a litheness in Harry's figure, and a handsome gentleness of demeanour that bespoke good blood, fine family, unmistakable valour and a determination when aroused, far more than any one would expect in one of his years.

To Count Vincento's great surprise the door was closed after him the moment he entered the apartment.

" Is this the man ?" the doctor asked his patient, in a half-whisper.

Lizzie Ashton half opened her drooping eye-lids for a

moment. She simply glanced at the stranger, and a tremor of horror and abhorrence passed through her frame.

"That is the wretch!" she calmly said, and sobbed aloud.

A growl as of some caged tiger fell upon the ears of all present!

At that moment, so great was his rage at the discovery of the miscreant, the enraged colonel burst open the wardrobe door and bounded towards his enemy!

"Villain!" he cried, and struck Count Vincento a terrible blow in the face.

The colonel's action was so precipitous that it fully disconcerted the doctor and landlord's plans.

The blow would have been followed by another but the count, smiling like a demon, wiped a few spots of blood from his lips, and, leaving the room, said jeeringly,

"Follow me!"

The doctor and landlord could not comprehend that the colonel would honour the ruffian with a personal encounter. They were stupefied therefore with surprise when the colonel ordered a hackney coach, and swore that he would have instant revenge.

By this time Darby had arrived with his hackney coach.

"Here, Darby, quick!" Harry exclaimed.

At that moment he jumped into the coach, and hurriedly said to the astonished coachman,

"Drive as fast as you can after those two hackney coaches that have just left the stable-yard."

For it should be explained that Colonel Ashton's rage had become so unmanageable and fierce that he had accepted all conditions of Count Vincento's challenge, and had started off alone to the field of combat, even without a surgeon, second or a witness.

Count Vincento, however, if we may so call that noted robber and one of Ivan the Terrible's followers, had been more fortunate, for he had prevailed upon two gentlemen to accompany and second him, as he said, "in an affair of honour with a famous old idiot, with whose daughter he had been a little too gallant on a long journey."

'Tis needless to say that had the two gentlemen known the true character of the imposter with whom they were riding, the count would have had to meet more than the old colonel in mortal combat.

Be that as it may, the three hackney coaches drove towards Hyde Park, and arrived there just at sunrise.

The coaches stopped beneath a group of trees inside the park.

Count Vincento and his two friends proceeded to a small group of trees, and were laughing and chatting quite merrily and thoughtlessly.

"Oh, this is not the *first* time, I can assure you," said Count Vincento, with an air of much indifference, "I have had several affairs of this kind. With the pistol I have few equals, with the sword no one can touch me!"

The old colonel perceived that Harry had followed him, and they stood talking to each other beneath a tree.

"If I am killed, young Mr. Percy, give this ring to my dear, darling Lizzie; it was her mother's gift to me. I am rich, and all will fall to her, but, if you can, be a friend to her through life; one who has already jeopardized his own life for her is far above all other worldly relations to me."

So saying he pressed Harry's hand several times.

One of Count Vincento's seconds approached the colonel.

"You have no friend present, colonel," he said, politely bowing.

The colonel reddened up to the temples as he remarked confusedly,

"Ah! in the hurry I forgot. Perhaps young Percy here will do me that honour?"

The rival second for a moment looked with pity, if not contempt, upon Harry, who, however, said, in a manly manner,

"Anything you desire, my dear colonel."

Before Harry left the colonel's side the old man said,

"If I fall, Harry Percy, do not tell Lizzie of it for some time, it would break her heart; she is the only child I ever had, and God knows I love her more than all the world besides."

In a few moments every preliminary was arranged.

It was agreed that they should fight with pistols at fifteen paces.

The weapons were loaded and handed to the combatants.

They took their distance.

One of the seconds, after a given signal, dropped a white handkerchief.

Two reports were simultaneously heard.

One is seen to fall!

The other stands bolt upright in his original position.

The first is stretched, a gory corpse, upon the green sward!

Harry rushes forward in grief and alarm.

Colonel Ashton is dead!

One of the count's seconds, having examined the colonel's fatal wound, walked across the sward, and highly complimented his principal's skill.

"Right through the heart, Count! You are a most skilful shot! Allow me to compliment you upon your extraordinary ability!"

"Yes," said the Count, with a triumphant smile, adding, with a chuckle, "I *ought* to know something of the use of weapons considering that I am one of my friend Ivan's favourite pupils."

"Ivan! Ivan! Who is *he*?" both his seconds asked. "I never heard of him."

"Indeed! never even heard of my friend Ivan?" Count Vincento replied, with a coarse laugh; "never even *heard* of my friend Ivan? Well, well, you have something to learn, my dear and very obliging friends," he said, with a contemptuous smile of triumph.

At that moment young Harry stood before the Count, and an angry altercation ensued.

"Take this *boy* away, or I shall be necessitated to chastise his impudence and want of manners. If you were a *man*, now, like your late principal who lies yonder, a monument of his own folly, I should call you out."

"Call *me* out," laughed Harry, boldly. "You have no need to do that. I am here, ready and willing, to try conclusions with you in *any* way!"

Count Vincento was full of rage, and attempted to strike Harry.

The latter, however, evaded the blow, and, to the astonishment of all present, he tripped the Count full on the grass.

After a stormy discussion, and many hard words on each side, Harry demanded satisfaction.

"Well, youngster, as you proudly call yourself a Percy, and as I should like to rid England of a few of that famous family, produce your swords, and I will accommodate you."

There was an air of confidence in Harry's manner that strangely contrasted to the livid paleness and quivering lips of his tall and powerful opponent.

"Well, then, if you, who are a man, powerful, strong, tall, and skilful, will not grant me the use of pistols, which would put both on an equality of distance and weapon, I accept swords, and trust my life, fortune and safety in the hands of Heaven."

This simple and heartfelt declaration was received with jeers by his opponent, who sarcastically asked,

"And who is your second, pray?" asked the Count, with an ineffable smile of contempt.

"*I* can find an honest man," was the quick reply; "that is more than *you* can say. Darby, my groom, will do for me."

Darby, hearing his own name mentioned, and supposing that he had to do a little, stepped forward and rolled up his sleeves, ready to box any one there present.

"But you have no swords?" Count Vincento replied, with a jeer. "We shall be obliged to postpone this affair until to-morrow."

"Not exactly, sir," Harry laughingly replied, "not even for one short half hour. There are weapons in my coach."

This announcement filled Count Vincento with surprise.

"I see you came prepared, then, boy," he said, pulling off his coat, and rolling up his shirt sleeves.

"I did as you observe," he said, going to his coach, and producing the swords. "There they are, gentlemen," he said, throwing them down at Count Vincento's feet, "See that they are both of equal length."

LAURA AND THE GIPSY GIRL VISIT THE ABBEY RUINS.—*See No. 3.*

Darby the groom, plucky, frolicsome and famous boxer as he was, was startled for the moment when he perceived the deadly intentions of his young master, and prayed and beseeched of him not to risk his life in combat with sharp-edged weapons, for a true British stable-boy, as he was, he had an inveterate hatred of everything save good hard knuckles and a stout arm to settle all disputes, and therefore he stood aghast at the shining, deadly swords.

"Be brave of heart, Darby. Remember I am a Percy, and will always hold myself as such in face of friend or foe."

"Have you any message to leave, sir, in case you should fall?" sobbed Darby, begging and beseeching Harry to allow *him* to settle the dispute. "For, look you here, Master Harry," said he, displaying his strong and muscular arm, "I can whop half-a-dozen sich as they is in a twinkling. I can give 'em one, two, and a buster, in no time!"

"My faithful servant, if I should die, tell my father all that you know concerning this affair, and add that I died as a Percy should, with his face to the foe, in the cause of woman's honour and virtue," said Harry, firmly.

Casting a look of affectionate regret at the dead body of his friend, he approached Count Vincento.

No. 2.

The Count contemptuously pointed his sword towards the colonel's gory body, as much as to say,

"*You* will also lie there, within a few moments."

Harry, with a smile upon his handsome, manly face, pointed his sword to heaven, saying aloud,

"In heaven alone I trust!"

Two of the seconds conducted each his principal to within four feet of one another.

They crossed swords.

The seconds withdrew, saying,

"Now, gentlemen!"

At that single simple word, both combatants stepped a pace forward, and their blades were quickly entangled up to the hilt.

"Retire," said Harry, all coolness and experience.

"I never retire before a silly *dog!*" was the response of the scowling, vindictive Count.

"Very well, sir, *I* do," was Harry's jovial remark, as he stepped back a single pace.

A few moments of frightful anxiety passed.

The swords twined round each other like snakes in deadly embrace.

Count Vincento took the offensive.

Harry was entirely on the defensive, and watched his adversary's eye with a bright, unflinching, hawk-like glance.

He was quiet, also remarkably cool, and a pleasant smile played around his mouth.

He acted, in truth, just as if he were at sword-play among his companions at school.

Count Vincento was not long in discovering that his boyish and unequal opponent was not much of a novice in the encounter.

The combat still continued, and each moment deepened in deadly interest.

Count Vincento was the only one that gave blows, but Harry was his equal, and parried them beautifully.

Darby, at one moment in tears, was now hysterical with joy, for his young master displayed consummate generalship and ability of the first order.

The groom, in truth, could not contain himself; he danced and capered about like a Merry Andrew, and, feeling much inclined himself to have a little "job" of some kind, as he facetiously called it, stepped up to Count Vincento's seconds, and, sparring off at them with his bare, brawny arms, would, in his own language, have "smashed them in no time," but that Harry perceived his servant's intentions and angrily called him away.

Darby's warlike demonstrations caused young Harry's eye to wander for a second.

"There!" said Count Vincento, in mock triumph, taking advantage of his youthful adversary's momentary distraction, "are you satisfied, young silly dog?"

His sword had grazed young Harry's arm, and blood flowed therefrom.

For a moment the brave youth spoke not, but, in a short time,

"There!" shouted Harry Percy, in return, as his sword struck his adversary's thigh, and drew a stream of blood.

The Count, who considered himself matchless with the sword, groaned aloud with fierceness, vexation and pain.

"'Tis nothing," he said, and rushed upon Harry with all the ferocity of an unchained tiger.

Harry smiled with confidence, but cold perspiration ran from the Count's brow profusely.

The witnesses, perceiving that blood had been drawn on either side, would have approached and interfered to stop the duel.

"No, no! go away!" roared the Count in terrific rage, and rushed at his opponent.

Harry, nothing loth to bring the contest to a close, followed up the Count with ardour, who gradually retreated.

"I thought you never retired," said Harry, carelessly.

Now tortured to the very quick with young Percy's taunt, becoming weak also from loss of blood, he bounded towards Harry with a dreadful lunge.

The point of his sword just grazed his left breast!

Harry nimbly stepped aside and parried the blow with all his strength.

The Count's bosom was for a single moment exposed and unguarded.

That single moment decided his fate!

In another second young Percy, quick of foot and sure of eye and aim, stepped one pace forward!

His sword pierced Count Vincento, and went up to its hilt!

The Count uttered a frightful oath and extended his arms!

His sword dropped from his hand!

He was alone prevented from falling by the weapon that had pierced him!

Young Percy withdrew his sword.

Count Vincento fell to the earth.

He was dead!

Some few moments after the duel the doctor cut open the count's clothes to examine the extent and nature of his wound.

All were astounded at what they then discovered!

He wore a coat of mail that was bullet proof!

The colonel's bullet, flattened against the chain armour, fell out into the doctor's hand!

Young Percy's sword had penetrated one of the loose and broken rings!

Hence the cowardly villain's death!

When the coat of mail was unbuckled all present were still more astonished at what they saw.

Upon his breast was branded

"THE SCORPION.
"I. T.
"CAPTAIN,"

Around which ran the motto,

"Day or night my aim is true!"

"What can you make of all this?" asked one, in pale surprise.

"Simply this," said young Percy, with a smile of contempt; "this *gentleman* was a *highwayman* of famed Ivan's band! He was thought a *brave* man, but has proved an odious scoundrel and *coward!*"

The seconds looked at each other in astonishment, and sneered at the young conqueror, but this was quickly perceived by the flushed and excited Darby, who rushed in between his master and them, and, "squaring off" in a determined manner, said, "If any of ye ain't quite satisfied, why, then, just drop your 'toasting forks' (alluding to the swords) and have a round or two wi' me, for, blow me, I should like to plant a bunch o' fives on some o' yer ugly snouts!"

Finding there was, as he termed it, "no game in the gents," he triumphantly caught up Harry in his arms, placed him in the coach, and waved his hat and shouted "H-o-o-ray!" until almost hoarse with his jubilant exertions.

CHAPTER VII.

THE MARVELLOUS ESCAPE OF CAPTAIN BLUE JACKET.

THE news of the arrest of "Blue Jacket" spread far and wide.

Bill Barry was feasted wherever he went, and, at the solicitation of the police authorities of Darlington, he stopped there, and consigned his prisoner to the old castle.

Blue Jacket took his rough treatment with stoical indifference, nor did he grumble when an old smith at the castle made his appearance, and with an assistant, began to iron the handsome young prisoner.

He was placed in one of the strongest cells in the castle, a jug of water and a loaf of bread were placed on an oak table beside him, and this was all that was allowed him.

Contrary to the expectations of all in the Castle, the prisoner betrayed no sorrow or despondency.

He whistled and sang all day long.

He seemed the most light-hearted fellow that ever lived, and took as much care of his toilet as if he were upon the point of taking an evening promenade with his sweetheart in the far-famed Mall or gardens of Old Vauxhall.

No one was allowed to see him.

His trial was to come off at no distant day.

"Well, Master Blue Jacket," said the gaoler, one morning as he went his rounds, "thou art as jolly as a sand boy, I see."

"Why shouldn't I be?" was the indifferent reply.

"Well, I don't know, lad; but if I were as near the gallows as thee, I think I'd take my prayer-book awhile now and then, and prepare for it," said the gaoler, seriously.

"Prayer book! Ha! ha!" Blue Jacket laughed. "I'm not a dead man yet."

"Ah, well! Master Blue Jacket, thou'rt a merry fellow, and it'll take a strong rope to hang thee wi', I think, if I'm not much mista'en. Since they have made thee leave off wearing that fancy blue cloth cloak and golden lace thou art not much better-looking than other folk, if thee *hast* long, black, curly hair; and, judging by thy long thin neck, I don't think Mister Jack Ketch 'll have much trouble in breaking it for thee, mister."

While the gaoler spoke the chaplain was announced, and entered the prisoner's cell.

The gaoler respectfully withdrew.

"Well, unhappy young man, I have come to see thee once

again ere you depart to London for execution, and hope you may be willing to hear my instructions. You have refused to listen to me time and time again; but I hope you will not do so now at least."

"Not a bit of it, Mr. Chaplain," Blue Jacket replied. "Thank you all the same. I would listen to you with pleasure; but you speak to me, and of me, as if I were a *dead* man instead of a *living* one. I'm not going to die yet, I can tell you," said Blue Jacket, with an air of merriment.

"Well, then, unhappy man, if you will not listen to *me*, if you have any objections to *me* personally, let me beg of you to accept the ministrations of another."

"Oh! certainly," Blue Jacket replied, with indifference. "*I* don't mind how many parsons come to see me; but one at a time is quite enough, I can tell you, for their faces are generally so long and cadaverous that it gives a man the horrors to look at them. Send whom you like, sir, but, if you please, somebody that's got a more pleasant countenance than yours."

"Alas! my heart and will have been good to serve you; but, as you wish it, there is a young travelling curate at the present moment staying with me who is very zealous. He has heard much of your notorious doings upon the king's highway, and feels ambitious to convert you from sin and wickedness, and prepare you for the scaffold," said the chaplain, with a pious groan.

"All right, then, send him when you like."

The minister departed.

The heavy doors were locked, and Blue Jacket began to sing loudly and merrily.

As best he could he amused himself by carving his name on the prison walls with a long nail.

He did the same upon the large, heavy oak table.

Having clambered up to his window bars, he looked out upon the beautiful face of the country, and like a young caged skylark he sighed to be on the wing again.

Towards evening the gaoler introduced a young clergyman, saying, as he opened the door,

"Blue Jacket, the Rev. Mr. Nelle Lovedale has come to convart ye. I hope you'll be werry serious and good."

The sinking sun shed its rays through the prison bars.

Blue Jacket sat in the shade with an averted face.

He seemed for once dejected and sorrowful.

"Mr. Lovedale! Oh, yes, I forgot," said Blue Jacket, dreamily and musing. "Take a seat, if you can find one; but——"

He turned his face round.

The young minister was weeping.

"Ah! look at that! look at that, you hardened young rascal," the gaoler said, as he moved towards the door to go out. "Look at that now. Why even the young minister is crying at your hardness of heart."

The gaoler thought it incumbent upon him to follow the example of the minister, and wiped his eye with the tail of his coat, and pulled a most ugly face before he retired.

The door had been but a moment shut, when the handkerchief dropped from the minister's face.

"What!" exclaimed Blue Jacket, as he narrowly scrutinised the features of the young minister. "Ellen Lovedale!"

"Hush!" said the minister, "or all is lost! I heard of your arrest. This is my disguise!"

Blue Jacket fell upon his knees and kissed the girl's hands again and again.

At that moment the cell door opened, and the gaoler entered!

The young minister turned upon the gaoler haughtily, saying,

"Can't you see that the prisoner is upon his knees, and silently praying with me? How dare you intrude upon our devotions?"

The gaoler blushed deeply, and retiring, said,

"Beg pardon, sir. Thought as how you couldn't make any good of him, and so I——"

"Well, my good man, leave us to our devotions, I beg."

"You see, sir, I goes off duty at eight o'clock, and another comes on for the night, then, sir,—and——"

"Begone, prattler," said the minister, "once more leave us in peace."

The door closed.

"*Another comes on at eight o'clock for the night!*" the minister mused. "Capital! The thing is easy; it could not be better! To-morrow night at this time you are free!"

Blue Jacket could do no more than fling his arms round Ellen's neck.

He kissed her a hundred times, and asked to hear of her strange adventures down from London; but she deferred the narration, saying,

"When you are once more free, and galloping towards London with a light heart, I will tell you all that has befallen the 'Fly-by-Nights;' but until then wait patiently. For the present, adieu!"

Blue Jacket kissed her again and again.

She departed!

A white cambric handkerchief was held to her eyes as she left.

"Poor young man!" said the gaoler, feelingly, "I'm afeered its no use o' talking to that hardened young willin." With that the outer gates were opened, and the Rev. Nelle Lovedale left the castle.

Blue Jacket was more jolly that night than ever.

He sang and danced, and rattled his chains, until the day turnkey thought his prisoner had gone crazy.

The moon arose, and shed its rays within his dismal cell!

When the tower clock solemnly tolled the hour of midnight, Blue Jacket listened at the door of his dungeon.

All was still!

Ellen Lovedale had given him two small saws and a file! She had concealed them in the leggings of her boots.

With these the highwayman began to work.

Before morning his irons and shackles were all but loose.

With little more labour he might have totally divested himself of them.

He knew, however, that his cell would be examined early in the morning.

He therefore left the rivets in the irons and shackles which kept them together, but could remove them at a moment's notice.

The gaoler visited his prisoner early on the morrow.

He found Blue Jacket intently engaged in reading a prayer-book.

Altogether his face and general demeanour wore an unusual and commandable aspect of sincere piety.

The bread and water were left on the table, and the unsuspecting turnkey departed.

During the day the Rev. Mr. Nelle Lovedale called, accompanied by the chaplain.

The latter was particularly struck by the altered demeanour of the hitherto obdurate prisoner.

Prayers were said, and hymns were sung, in which Blue Jacket's voice could be heard high above, and louder than the rest.

It was, however, observed by the chaplain, and with evident pleasure, that his young brother minister and the prisoner often hung their heads very low, and applied handkerchiefs to their eyes!

Such contrition and happiness the worthy chaplain did not expect to see in one who had so stoutly resisted all his previous exhortations and admonitions.

Whether the pocket handkerchiefs were to dry up penitential or joyous tears, we leave our attentive readers to surmise.

Suffice it to say, however, that when the chaplain offered up a final prayer, the Rev. Nelle Lovedale and the prisoner knelt side by side with handkerchiefs to their eyes, and any one could have easily observed how the frames of both individuals heaved and shook with emotion!

The chaplain and his brother minister took their departure, shaking Blue Jacket cordially by the hand.

The minister had not departed more than a moment when the prisoner burst out into a quiet laugh.

He shook again with merriment. The gaoler entered, however, and Blue Jacket resumed his prayer-book very devoutly.

"Well, I'm very glad they've done ye *some* good," said he, "but ye be an unkimmon rogue, Master Blue Jacket, for it takes a brace of parsons to convart *thee*! They be coming again to-night, so the young 'un told me, so prepare thyself well, for thee hasna many days to live, so I hear."

With that the gaoler departed, and Blue Jacket grinned. "Both coming again to-night, eh? Why, what does all this mean?"

He could not make it out at all.

At half-past seven precisely the Rev. Mr. Lovedale arrived in full clerical attire, for he was going to administer the sacrament, he said, and was ushered into the dungeon.

The gaoler stood outside.

What passed within he knew not.

He heard them singing a hymn together, and thought the prisoner was becoming amazingly pious all at once, judging from the loudness of his voice.

Had he seen all that was then transpiring it would have opened his eyes considerably.

While they were singing a hymn, the Rev. Mr. Lovedale was unloosing the rivets of Blue Jacket's shackles.

This done, he lifted up his skirts and produced therefrom a second suit of clerical vestments.

Blue Jacket put them on, wig and all!

The transformation was so great that no one could have detected him.

When Mr. Lovedale pulled up his clerical skirts Blue Jacket was much surprised to find that the reverend gentleman had on a suit of clothes similar to his own in every respect!

When, therefore, Blue Jacket had put on the suit of clericals which had been brought for him, Mr. Lovedale pulled off his own, and hid them under the cot bed!

He then approached the cell door, saying aloud, "Well, then, my friend, as you desire it, I will leave the Castle, and bring the regular chaplain to see you; he only lives a hundred yards from the gates."

His voice attracted the gaoler's attention.

He opened the cell door!

Blue Jacket, in his clerical attire, and with a handkerchief to his face, passed out.

The gaoler bowed, peeped in, and seeing the prisoner sitting in his chair in a dark part of the cell, said gruffly,

"Well, you are a trouble to 'em!" and locked the door.

The moment that was done Ellen Lovedale resumed her clerical attire.

She rattled Blue Jacket's chains, occasionally, however, to deceive the gaoler's ears, but could not help suppressing smothered laughter the while.

In half-an-hour the chaplain arrived, and was ushered into the cell.

The gaoler did not enter, but left the door ajar, and went away.

"Where is the prisoner?" asked the chaplain, in surprise.

"Oh, he's gone into the governor's room for a few moments, he was just now sent for. He won't be long."

The chaplain, suspecting no harm, sat down and sighed over Blue Jacket's depravity.

"Wait a moment, reverend sir," said Mr. Lovedale. "I will go and fetch the prisoner. He desires much to see you ere he goes to London."

The chaplain made no reply, but opened his prayer-book, and sat reading.

In a moment Ellen Lovedale closed the door, turned the key noiselessly in the lock, and departed.

"Good evening, sir," said the gaoler, respectfully, as he passed him in the Castle yard.

"Good evening," was Mr. Lovedale's reply, as he went out. "The prisoner is deeply engaged with your good and pious chaplain. I have done all I can for the poor ignorant and depraved young highwayman. Don't disturb them in their devotions for at least half-an-hour."

The outer gates were opened!

He departed!

In half-an-hour the gaoler went to the cell door, and heard the chaplain shouting out at the top of his voice,

"Murder! Thieves! Let me out! Let me out!"

The door was opened.

Lo! Great was the surprise of all!

The prisoner had escaped!

The truth instantly flashed upon the minds of all.

The alarm was sounded all over the Castle, and mounted men sent in pursuit.

'Twas all in vain.

At that moment Ellen Lovedale, in man's attire, was furiously galloping along the road to London.

By her side rode Blue Jacket, laughing.

CHAPTER VIII.

TREACHERY—THE SPY IN SOCIETY—THE INTRIGUE—THE DEFAMATION—THE DUEL OF REVENGE - THE RESULT— THE SORCERER IS DEFIED.

THE news of Harry Percy's duel with the famous Count Vincento, and its successful issue, filled Castle Percy with surprise.

Earl Percy, old as he might be, and infirm, was astounded!

That his youngest son, a mere boy, should have rescued a beautiful maiden from a watery grave, afterwards act as second to Colonel Ashton, and then avenge his death at the sword's point, were matters and facts that fairly stupefied the delighted old nobleman.

When Harry's sister, Lady Laura, heard of it, however, she turned deadly pale.

She tottered from weakness, and retreated from the presence of her father.

Why was this?

Had she, a fair and beautiful young girl, an earl's daughter, ever aught to say or do with Count Vincento?

Had not her brother Harry informed them all that he had rendered his king and country a service, in ridding the world of a noted seducer and rogue, who under an assumed name, had crept into the best society, although at the same time he belonged to, and was a sworn member of, an infamous band of thieves and cut-throats, under the leadership of Ivan the Terrible?

Be that as it may, the young and seductive Laura, trembled in every limb as she listened to the reading of her brother's letter.

When she retired to her chamber she bitterly wept.

No one was nigh to witness her grief, save Jessie, her faithful maid.

Jessie was a foundling, and when but a babe had been discovered in Percy Park, near to a spot where a gipsy encampment had stood the night before.

She had been well cared for, and grew up a beautiful girl, with large, dark flashing eyes, a nut-brown complexion, long black hair, and a bewitching figure.

As she knelt, or sat at the feet of her young mistress, she gazed long and ardently at the weeping maid, and said,

"Dear young mistress, your tears and sorrow give me pain. You have always been good and kind to me, a poor, friendless orphan. We have been reared together, and have been constant companions, and although I am but a servant and slave, you have ever called me your sister Jessie. As your poor slave, then, or as your sister Jessie, let me beg and beseech you to confide to me the secret of your sorrows."

"The name of that accursed wretch fills me with horror," said Lady Laura, in deadly pallor.

"What name, fair lady?" asked the gipsy maid, in surprise.

"What name?" said Laura, with a trembling lip. "why, that of Count Vincento, and of his ruthless master, Ivan the Terrible!"

"I have heard of the frightful doings of Ivan the Terrible on sea and land, my own heart's mistress, but never, until now, of Count Vincento's. Was he not one of the leaders of fashion in London?" asked Jessie, with distended eyes.

"He was, alas! for my happiness; but never, until now, could I believe that he was in league with Ivan and his terrible band. But this I know," said Laura, with trembling lips, "Count Vincento was a murderer, and——"

"Murderer?" asked Jessie, in alarm.

"Murderer! Aye, a most foul, cruel assassin! If you doubt me—if, hitherto, you could never assign a cause for my melancholy and sadness, listen to my painful story, and of one incident of Ivan the Terrible's band."

After a pause, Lady Laura began with a trembling voice :—

"My aunt," said Laura, "went to Paris, to attend a lawsuit she had there, and for health's sake my noble father permitted me to accompany her. She went out each day, thinking it would enable her to influence her judges. In the evening we took pleasant walks, and there I often met a distinguished-looking gentleman of decidedly English appearance, though named Count Vincento.

"He was my constant shadow!

"His presence became to me intolerable, and from that time my indifference was changed to aversion."

"Was he a person likely to cause such a sentiment?" said Jessie.

"Why should you ask?" inquired Lady Laura. "You were too young to have remarked anything; but do you recollect my cousin Richard, the son of my father's brother?"

Jessie contracted her eyebrows, and replied in a short manner,

"Yes; he was a young naval officer. When he returned from sea, he usually spent most of his leisure time at Percy House, in London. He was a lieutenant, in the frigate ' Macedonian ;' have you heard from him lately?"

"When we left Paris, his mother was very uneasy respecting his silence. He is dead!" said Lady Laura with desperate calmness.

"Dead!" exclaimed Jessie, with astonishment.

"Count Vincento killed him!"

"Is your aunt ignorant of this?"

"Listen. The time is come for me to disclose all to you. You know I had been brought up with Richard. When a child I loved him as a brother; but as years rolled on I looked upon him as my future husband, or, rather, I might say these two sentiments were blended together into one; but although you were my constant companion, you were, then, young, and our love, no doubt, escaped you."

"To speak the truth, Lady Laura, I recollect something, which ought to have enlightened me on the subject. But can it be possible that Richard is dead? When and where did it happen?"

"Listen. I had been promised marriage by him. Can you now comprehend my aversion to the count?"

"Yes."

"Vincento redoubled his pursuit of me. Informed of our residence in Paris, he tried, with great perseverance, to form a connection with those who might be of assistance to my aunt in her law affairs. He did so, and gained so much influence with them, that he was soon in a position to be of the greatest service to my aunt.

"Finding his way thus clear, he one day declared his intention to my aunt of lodging at the same hotel. The reception I gave him was very chilling; but his manner was so fascinating that, by flattery, he showed my aunt how greatly he could assist her in the progress of her suit, and she invited him to visit us as often as he thought proper. On leaving the room he cast a very significant look at me. He did this in order that he might be able to approach me more intimately on the next occasion.

"I expressed suspicions as to his sincerity; but my aunt replied that I was crazy, and also that we should avail ourselves of the Count's kind offers since he would be so advantageous to us.

"My aunt had been very handsome in her youth. She was then only forty years of age.

"The Count perceived one day that she received with great pleasure some little gallantries which he addressed to her in jest. He increased his attentions so much that in a short time she could not do without him.

"He would accompany us everywhere : to the theatre, or walking or riding.

"I remarked to my aunt that he being young and rich this intimacy might compromise me.

"Her reply was, that I was quite wrong to alarm myself. She was a widow and free ; the Count had told her he loved her, adding that he took deep interest in the law suit because it gave him an opportunity of enjoying her society.

"I wished to make some observations; she would not listen to me, but broke out into a tirade about the vanity of girls, and reproached me with ever having believed for a moment that the Count bestowed a thought upon me.

"He often sent minstrels under our window, saw us every day, and constantly gave us similar bouquets, in order, as he told my aunt, that my self-love might not be wounded.

"One day, finding me alone, he made a declaration of love. Considering as a merit in my eyes the ability with which he had deceived my aunt, he thought I should admire and feel kindly disposed towards him for this enormous sacrifice."

"And was your aunt informed of this avowal of Count Vincento?"

"Yes; that very evening I told her all!"

"Then you unmasked him!" said Jessie, with a bright eye.

"Jessie! you cannot tell the vanity and weakness of women!"

"What! would she not believe you?"

"Yes, she did; and that same evening our door was closed against the Count.

"He guessed what had happened, and wrote a long letter to my aunt.

"The next day she received him more kindly than before! When he had left the house, my aunt came and scolded me very severely; she declared I was jealous of the Count's love for *her*, and that I had calumniated him in order to have him excluded from the house."

"She must have been mad!" said the maid, with a curling lip.

"Matters resumed their usual course. The Count never spoke of love to me, still he spent whole days with us.

"On the 14th of May!—ah! I shall never forget that date !—my aunt told me that the noise of the court-yard gate of the hotel disturbed her so much that she would exchange apartments with me. The room, which until then I had occupied, looked into the street, and had a balcony!

"What I have to add is fearful! On that day we had been out for a long drive in the carriage, accompanied by the Count.

"When we returned, we sat together until very late in the evening, my aunt appearing very much pre-occupied. At length we retired, and went to bed!"

Here Laura turned deadly pale, shuddered, and then continued in a broken voice :—

"The next day I expressed a wish to see my aunt as usual, when her maid, with an embarrassed air, told me that she was indisposed, and could not see either me or any one.

"Upon returning to my own apartment a stranger inquired for me ; a dark, pale man gave me a letter without uttering a syllable. I cannot tell what I thought or felt, but a tremour ran through my veins. Upon opening the letter I found a ring which I had given to Richard."

"And the letter—the letter?"

"Was from Richard; he was dying!"

"From your cousin Richard?"

"Yes. The words it contained seemed to me to be written in characters of blood! They were these,

"' I have been in Paris two days. I know all! I saw, this very night, Count Vincento descending from your balcony, after which you closed the window. I fought with him instantly. I sought death and he has given it to me. Be thou accursed! You shall know more when you return to London. Conceal from my mother the story of my death. My sight is failing. I am dying fast!

"' R.'"

"And nothing more?" asked Jessie, in alarm.

"Not a word," Laura replied, with an agonised expression.

"What a mystery!" said Jessie. "Who, then, could have appeared at your chamber window?"

"Did I not tell you that my apartments were occupied by my aunt that very evening? No doubt the Count had obtained a rendezvous from her in order to serve his wicked designs. You understand me now? She is exactly my height, dark as I am, and thus was my dear lost cousin fatally deceived!"

"Oh, how horrible!"

"Upon reading this letter I was almost mad; I felt as if in a dream. A friend of his told me the rest, which was this: On